SNOW BLITZ

GRIDIRON LEGACY

AVA SUTTON

COMPASS PRESS

ISBN-13: 979-8-9999643-4-2

For Jeannine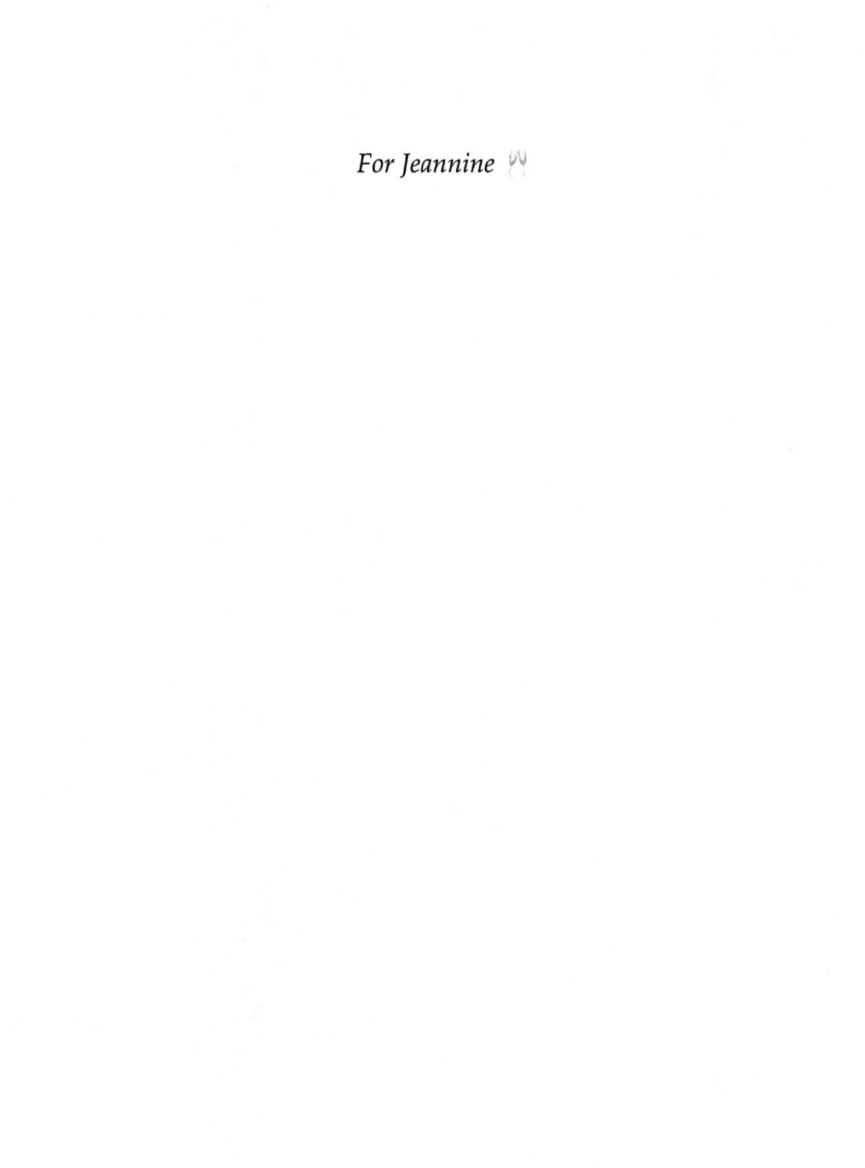

CHAPTER
ONE

LIAM

Why am I standing on a rooftop in the middle of Winter, freezing my balls off? I did not sign up for this. I thought coming to some posh wedding meant we would at least be, you know, comfortable. I'd take the heat and humidity of New Orleans over this.

I came up to New York City for one of my college teammates' weddings. Brandon was my roommate when I transferred to Michigan after I left Walker. He and his new wife live in New York since he plays for the Titans, so they got married at some fancy hotel in midtown during a bye week.

Coming up here also gave me a good excuse to escape a little drama of my own too. Last week, I broke it off with someone I had been seeing because I need to stay focused on football right now. Too bad for Sabine, she thought our relationship was more serious than it was ever going to be.

Her texts have been coming in more frequently over the last few days, including two today, so yeah, I'll probably have to change my number when I get back from New York. I have a feeling Sabine won't leave me alone otherwise.

Trying to warm myself up, I take a hefty gulp of my Macallan Eighteen. Sure, there are heating lamps placed strategically around the rooftop with a glass wraparound to cut the wind, but it's still fucking cold. It's only supposed to be a short cocktail hour up here, then we'll go to the main dining room for dinner, but I've been standing in this same spot for close to an hour under one of the heaters. If I had been better prepared and maybe worn a thicker coat, I wouldn't be acting like a pussy about the whole thing.

Glancing around, I take in the all-white wedding theme. Even we, the guests, were asked to wear white. It almost feels like we're in a white-out blizzard...inside a snow globe...that you can't get out of, because it also started snowing about ten minutes ago. *Fuck, I'm trapped in this snow globe world and starting to feel claustrophobic now.*

A few of my old college teammates from Michigan are hanging around, but almost everyone brought a date, except me. They've tried to include me, and I can carry on a conversation with the best of them, but I'm just not feeling it tonight. I'll probably duck out after we eat.

They're all great guys, but I miss my guys from Walker. We're all on our own paths now, too, but we try to see each other now and then. Especially Archie Griffith. He's my best friend and the one I talk to the most.

My friends are either in the league now, too, or will be soon. And they're all falling in love. Not only are they falling in love, but they're getting married and, in Archie's case, having babies.

I pull out my phone because now I really miss them. *Damn, I'm feeling sappy.* I take a quick selfie and send it off to Archie, Beck, and Casey.

> Liam: Wishing you guys were in NYC with me this weekend.

> Beck: Aren't you at a wedding?

Liam: Well, yeah, but it's kinda boring.

Casey: Dude, I can't travel right now. We had a game today. You know this.

Archie: Sorry, buddy. I have a game tomorrow and Emma is studying this weekend, so I'm on baby duty. Heading down to the ranch for a bit so Em can have the house quiet.

Liam: You guys suck. You should have come with me.

Casey: You love us.

Liam: Unfortunately. Assholes.

Archie: Have a good time. Maybe get laid or something. One of the bridesmaids?

Beck: Text us later. Charlie just got here and says hi.

Liam: Tell Little King I said hey.

Beck: Soon to be Linson.

Casey: Still a King right now.

Liam: Fine. I'll send you pictures of all the fun things I'll be doing in New York. Without y'all.

Archie: Fun things to do... you mean pussy, right?

Liam: Any girl I meet tonight in New York would be strictly a hook up.

Archie: Don't do anything I wouldn't do. HA! Text me later, Pitzy.

I laugh, then drop my phone into my pocket, and when I look up, I see a woman with long dark brown hair standing next to the bundled-up bride in a long, bright red coat. I'm guessing she didn't get the "all white" memo. Then I see my buddy, Aaron Muldoon, walk up to her. He places a hand on the small of her back, and when she turns her head to look up at him, I almost drop my whisky glass.

I've seen some beautiful women in my life, but she is unbelievably stunning, and I can't even see her whole face yet. But then they turn and walk away from the bride, and I get to see her head on. She's got long shiny dark brown hair that looks like silk, with piercing blue eyes, a perfectly symmetrical nose, and her lips...*fuck me*. They're full and painted in bright red lipstick that matches her coat.

They're walking toward me now, and he leans down to say something to her that makes her laugh, and I'm done for. By the time they reach me, I've managed to pick my jaw up off the floor and compose myself enough that I don't look like an idiot.

"Sup, man. How's it going? Good to see you." Aaron reaches his hand out and pulls me in for a bro-hug.

"Muldoon, good to see you. How's New York treating you?" I ask him, but glance her way.

"Good, good. The season's been—" Aaron stops talking when he looks behind me. "Oh, shit, I gotta go say hi to someone, I'll be right back." Aaron looks at the woman as he walks away.

"Okay then. No problem. I'll just stand here by myself freezing, but cool, cool." She tucks a piece of her hair behind her ear.

"Right?" I chuckle. "Whose idea was this? I mean, it does look incredible, but these heating lamps aren't doing a whole lot to cut the chill."

She straightens her arms and holds her hands out. "Picture this...New York City, it's snowing, love and Christmas magic are in the air, but I feel like I'm standing in a cryo chamber."

"Ha! Pretty close to the truth there. You ever been in one?" I tilt my head toward her.

She nods, smirking. "Oh yeah. I'm a fan, but this is like really kinda crazy."

"It really is. I was just thinking about leaving after dinner. My hotel room is calling my name. I'll need a good thaw out after this. Until then, a stiff drink helps." I lift my glass to my lips and take another pull of my whisky.

"Whatever you have in that, I might need some to warm up." She tips her head toward my glass.

"Do you want some of this while I go get you a drink?" I hand it out to her.

"Hmm...risky taking a drink from a stranger. But you look like a trustworthy guy, and Aaron seems to know you, so why not?" She takes my offered glass and takes a sip. "Nice. Macallan. Eighteen?"

My mouth drops open, then I shut it so I can form words. "You know your whisky?"

"Mmm. I do. My father is a big fan. I also love a good brandy." She hands it back to me. "So, are you here on the bride or groom's side? Guessing the groom since you know Aaron?"

"Groom. I know Brandon from Michigan. Think I was more of a courtesy invite than anything else. We were roommates, but not incredibly close."

She laughs a warm sound that blends with the music. "I came as Aaron's plus one. His girlfriend missed her flight, so I said I'd keep him company. That said, he's more interested in working the room and catching up with people."

I smile. "Yeah, he always was a social guy. Always the life of the party. Even when it's freezing."

She takes my drink from my hand and lifts it slightly. "The whiskey helps." She takes a sip, and I take it back from her, lifting it in my own cheers. "To questionable decisions and good whiskey."

She laughs, and there's a devilish twinkle in her eyes. I'm mesmerized by them until lights begin to brighten behind her in various shades of red, blue and purple. I move to the side to see where they're coming from.

"It's the lights at Saks," she states, and I arch a brow. She further explains, "The holiday lights show at Saks Fifth Avenue. The sparkling wonderland of lights and music that graces the building's facade every ten minutes." There's a turn in her voice as she realizes I have no idea what she's talking about. "I forgot you're not from here."

I grin. "Midwestern boy. Kansas born and raised. How did you guess?"

"I hear the hint of twang. Have you ever been to New York City at Christmas?" She rubs her gloved hands together.

I shake my head. "I have not. And, unfortunately, I'm only here for the weekend and spending the better part of it in my own snowglobe of New York City instead of exploring it."

"Too bad because a guy like you could get into a lot of trouble in this city."

I'm just about to say something when a woman wearing a headset starts to speak. "Excuse me, everyone, can I have your attention please? Thank you so much for your patience tonight. There was a minor water issue that we're working to resolve. We should be able to go in shortly. In the meantime, we'll be bringing more appetizers out for you to enjoy. And don't forget to grab a drink at the bar." She waves her hand, then spins around and walks over to the bride and groom.

I glance over at this angel in red, and she meets my gaze.

"I have an idea." She says, grinning.

"Oh yeah, what's your idea?" I move in a little closer to her.

"How invested are you in staying here?"

I mean, is this a trick question? "Uhh, not very."

"I..." She starts to say something, then stops.

"I..." I prompt her.

She laughs. "I was going to say, do you want to get out of here? Let me show you what a Manhattan Christmas is like."

Fuck. Yes. "Absolutely. But I don't even know your name."

She tilts her head to the side. "Let's go with…Vixen. And you can be…Blitzen."

"What? Why?" I chuckle.

"Because it's fun and Christmas is magical." She holds out her hand to me. "What do ya say, Blitzen? You wanna go make some Christmas magic with me?"

I place my hand in her small one. "Lead the way, Vixen."

CHAPTER
TWO

LIAM

When we get to the elevator, she drops my hand and presses the button for the lobby.

"So where are we going?" I ask her.

"Well, since we're already at Rockefeller Center, we can take a minute to admire the tree, if you haven't yet." She looks at me, brows raised.

"I didn't even know it was here." I shrug.

"Right, right. So, we'll do that first. It's like a must on the list." She pulls out her phone and taps something that I can't see.

"You really aren't going to tell me your name?" I place my hand on her lower back and scoot in closer to her. I can smell her perfume; it's light but smells like the roses in my mom's garden.

"Nah, I don't think I will. And don't tell me yours."

"Are you a felon on the run or something?"

"Maybe, maybe not. Honestly, I just want to have mindless fun tonight."

"Life's been crazy lately?" I ask, but actually, it's like a statement of my own. Between traveling, workouts, game play, game strategy, contracts, deals, managing time with friends and family... I've been a little stressed myself.

"You could say that the real world can get a little intense sometimes..Let's just have fun together tonight. I never get to see the city from a tourist's view, so this will be fun for me. Let's live in the fantasy." She reaches around her back and takes my hand in hers again, just as the doors to the elevator open.

"Okay, let's live in the fantasy." I squeeze her hand, and she looks over her shoulder at me and winks.

When we walk out of the building, we're face to face with St Patrick's Cathedral. I know it from every Manhattan Christmas movie I've seen, but I only glance at it as she pulls me down Fifth Avenue and toward those lights I saw from the rooftop. Saks Fifth Avenue is blaring *Carol of the Bells* while an incredible light display moves across the block-wide department store. We stop walking, and Vixen places her hand on my chin and turns my face away from the music, and I'm instantly staring at a Christmas postcard.

Down an alley of lighted angels is the Rockefeller tree with the iconic building standing grand behind it. Television doesn't do it justice. It really is pretty incredible. I would say it stands at least seventy to seventy-five feet tall, with what looks like millions of glittering colored lights.

"What do you think?" she asks.

I shrug. "I thought it'd be bigger."

Her bottom lip pokes out, and I grin, showing her I'm just messing around with her. She gives me a playful shove in the chest.

We make our way through the crowded concourse and around the upper ledge that looks down at the ice skating rink below us, with families and couples spinning around the loop. Some sections are almost mob-like, so I pull our joined hands toward me, forcing her to my side in a protective stance. I don't want to lose her, and I most certainly don't like the way some of the men stare at her as we pass. She may have a firecracker personality, but she's a vixen in heels, and almost everyone we pass has taken notice.

It isn't lost on me the way she snakes a hand behind my suit jacket and clings to me as we walk to the base of the tree. When I finally release her, she still stands close to me.

"So, Vixen, are you a born and raised New Yorker?"

She looks up at me and smiles. "Both sides of my family have been here for generations. And other than my time in college, I've lived here my whole life and will probably die here."

"Well, that's kind of morbid, especially standing here in front of this beautiful Christmas tree." I chuckle.

She smacks my stomach playfully. "I guess you're right, but I just mean I love my city. New York is the greatest city in the world."

"You aren't biased or anything, right?" I laugh and put my arm around her waist. Sure, I'm a flirt, but I don't usually feel so at ease with anyone so soon. But there is something about her that just makes me want to touch her.

"Okay, funny guy, let's keep going. Christmas magic awaits!" She takes my hand in hers again. "Oh, wait. Let's take a selfie. Are you good with that?"

"Totally, but I want you to send them to me too."

"I will at the end of the night. Deal?" She releases my hand and pulls her phone out of her pocket.

"Deal," I say, leaning down so my head fits in the frame, and wrap my arms around her waist from behind.

She tilts her head toward mine, the tree perfectly placed behind us, and snaps a picture. We're both smiling, and look like a candy cane with my white outfit and her red coat. And now I want to be twisted up with her like a candy cane, in the warmth of my hotel room.

"Okay, let's roll," she says. We link our hands and start walking down 50th St. "Are you cold?"

"Nah, I'm good. It's warmer down here than it was on the

rooftop. My body temperature usually runs hot. Are you good?" I ask her. "You're in fancy clothes."

"Yep, I'm good." She lifts up her long coat and reveals ankle-length red pants.

"Huh, I assumed you had a dress on under that coat."

"I'm not a fan of dresses. I'm too antsy for dresses. I like to be able to move around without worrying I'm flashing my ass at everyone, you know?" She smirks.

I chuckle and nod. "I get it. I hate it when I flash my ass at strangers. I mean, I have a nice ass, don't get me wrong, but I'm selective on who I want oogling it."

"I bet that happens to you a lot. I can't see what's under your coat, but if it looks anything like the rest of you, it must be nice." She winks at me.

This girl. I love that she's not timid or shy, and she's not trying to impress me. She's very…real.

"I think you're flirting with me, Vixen."

"I just might be, Blitzen." She teases, making us both laugh.

"Are you gonna tell me where we're going next, or is it a surprise? I don't know where I'm going, so pretty much everything will be unknown to me. I've only seen some things on TV or in movies."

We get to 6th Ave and make a right, crossing the street toward the lights of Radio City Music Hall.. There's a crowd of people standing outside the building. "Is there a show tonight?"

"Yep, the Radio City Christmas Spectacular. I know you've heard of the Rockettes back in Kansas. But that's not where we're going. I could probably find a way to get us tickets, but I don't think you're the kind of guy who wants to sit down for two hours when you can rock around the city. Unless you really want to see the show." She looks up at me, questioningly.

"I'll go wherever you take me. I'm a pretty easy guy. I'm letting a snow kissed angel drag me around a city I could get lost in, so I'll just keep holding your hand." I squeeze her hand and smile down at her.

"Snow kissed angel. I like that." She returns my smile, and I swear her eyes sparkle.

When we reach the corner in front of Radio City Music Hall, we cross the street again. There's a large fountain with giant ornaments sitting in the water.

"Let's take our next few selfies here. We'll get one with the ornaments behind us, then we'll get another one with the theater behind us." She looks around, then seems to find a spot.

"Okay, sounds good. Do they do the ornaments every year, or is it different every season?" I ask, looking around at the various sizes in the fountain.

"Every year. They're kind of iconic. You can't do Christmas in New York without posing with the city's biggest balls."

I raise an eyebrow. "Big claim."

She smirks. "Hey, it's tradition. And selfies are the perfect tourist memento. You don't just remember what you saw, you remember who you were with when you saw it."

I grin. "So basically, photographic evidence that I met a snow kissed angel and her giant balls?"

She bursts out laughing. "Careful, Blitzen. That caption writes itself."

I move to stand behind her again and wrap my arms around her waist, and this time, I rest my chin on her shoulder. "Ready."

To a passerby, we probably look like a couple who's been together for a while. We're definitely not acting like strangers. She seems just as comfortable with me as I am with her. That has to mean something. Sexy, unpredictable and funny. *What are the chances that I meet my dream girl at a wedding? In another city. In a different state.*

"Okay, let's move over there to get a better shot of Radio City behind us." She points to an area a little further down the fountain pool.

"Yes, ma'am." I take a minute to appreciate the sway of her hips as she walks.

We take another selfie, then she taps out a text on her phone. "How do you feel about ice skating?"

"Ice skating?" I thumb back toward Rockefeller Center. "You mean where we just–"

"Ugh. No. That's a tourist trap that will have you standing online for two hours for a ten minute skate. I have somewhere better and we don't have to wait in line."

"Uh…I could do that. Although it's been years since I've been on skates. Not really a big thing where I'm from. I'm not sure the dress socks I'm wearing, or the heels you're wearing, are going to work with the skates, though." I point to her shoes. "Or that I'm dressed like a human snowflake in a white suit."

"It would be an issue if you didn't fill that suit out so well."

I smirk, and she rolls her eyes.

"Please don't fake modesty with me. We've known each other far too long for that."

"You mean—what—thirty minutes?"

"Our friendship is eternal." She sways playfully from side to side, then lifts a hand toward the street. "Oh! We're making a stop first. Come on, my driver's picking us up on the corner." She takes my hand, and I thread my fingers with hers. Even though she's wearing gloves, I can still feel the heat from her hand.

"Your driver? Can't we just grab a cab?" I ask her.

"Nah, it'll be faster for my driver to get us."

We continue walking, and a three-person jazz band is playing Christmas carols. A saxophonist, a drummer and a bass player are jamming to *Let It Snow*. It's an upbeat melody, the kind you'd hear on a Michael Bublé album. I tug on her hand toward the jazz trio in front of a pair of towering candy canes wrapped in glittering lights, and she looks up at me.

"Dance with me?" I may not be the most romantic guy, but I'm feeling this with her, and honestly, I just want to hold her again. But this time, I want to look in her eyes while I do.

She laughs, half in protest, half surrender.

I pull her into me, and then I wrap her arms over my shoulders, then I wind mine around her waist, moving in closer. We sway on the sidewalk, moving together to the music's lazy swing. Her heels slipping once as I move to spin her and bring her back. She laughs, seemingly at the absurdity of this moment – strangers embarking on an adventure in the city, yet stop to dance for no reason at all.

I swing her again and dip her this time. When I pull her up, we're so close our noses are practically touching. I can still smell the whiskey and mint on her breath, and it's making me want to taste her lips.

"Still want to go ice skating?" My eyes flit between her eyes and her mouth.

She nods and swallows. "Uh, yeah. But…I think we'll make a stop first."

I raise a brow at her innuendo. She laughs. "Looks like I found someone on Santa's naughty list. Get your mind out of the gutter. Looks like you really need to get on the ice and cool down."

"Hmm, you think I'll like it, do you? Even though I haven't been on skates in years?" I smirk.

"I think you'll hold your own. You look pretty…athletic to me." Our eyes meet, and the corners of her mouth tug up.

She doesn't seem to know who I am, but she knows I'm friends with Aaron, so her guess is right. I'm just surprised she isn't saying anything about it or asking me how Aaron and I know each other.

"In fact, I am pretty athletic. But I still need you to hold my hand until I get used to it." I move in just a little closer. I'm an inch away from taking her lips when a horn honks loudly next to us, drowning out the music.

She pulls away. "That's our ride. We should get going." Her hand comes up, and she tucks a piece of hair behind her ear.

"Okay, yeah. On to the next adventure." I follow behind her to the waiting car.

CHAPTER
THREE

LIAM

We pull up to a building that says Bergdorf Goodman a few minutes later, since it's just a few blocks away. We probably could have walked there faster, to be honest. There are some Christmas decorations in the windows that look like something out of an old-fashioned movie.

"We're going shopping?" I ask her.

"We're going to run inside for a few essential items." She scoots closer to me so we can get out the same side of the car.

"Are they still open?" I look out the window and then turn to her. "I'm actually staying at The Plaza, which I think is right down the street. I can just run to my room and change."

"The clock is ticking to get some socks and a pair of gloves for you." She pushes me a little. "Open the door, it's time to scoot."

"Okay, let's do it." I exit the car and hold the door open. I take her hand as she climbs out of the car.

"Thank you, Blitzen. Let's go get what we need to continue

our night of fun." Her eyes are sparkling again, and she acts like she's walking into a candy store.

"You like to go shopping?" I chuckle.

"Sure, but I'm more excited about what comes after the shopping. Okay, let's split up and go get what we need and meet back here in ten minutes. Does that give you enough time to find what you need?" She turns to face me.

"Just tell me where I need to go and I'll get it done. I'm a guy, so the first pair I see will work." I hold out my hands and smile.

"Right, okay. You go that way." She points behind me. "I'm heading this way." She throws a thumb over her shoulder.

We both take off quickly, and I make my way to the men's department and quickly spot the accessories. I pull a pair of light grey wool socks off the fancy table, then move to the next section, where hats and gloves are displayed. I'll skip the hat, but I grab a pair of grey leather gloves. Considering I'm wearing all white, I feel like the grey will blend in a little better than black would. I mean, I'm no fashionista, but I can practically hear my mom's voice in my head, leading me to the grey. I guess I'll find out soon enough if I made the right color choices.

I don't know what I'm doing here. Bergdorf's, of all places. Holiday chaos, lights flashing, music on the speakers. I left a wedding an hour ago. *A wedding.* The kind of thing I usually bail on before dessert. And now I'm in Midtown, chasing after a woman I barely know. That's not me. I don't chase. I don't...do this.

Commitments have never been my thing. Never wanted to owe anyone anything. First, my focus was on college and football, with any free time devoted to my friends. Now, my pro career is my top priority. Not that Vixen is looking for a commitment. Actually, this spontaneous night in New York is exactly what I look for in a woman. And yet, I'm already wondering what happens at the end of this night. What happens tomorrow...

I should walk away–catch a cab, get back to the hotel, and

keep the night simple before I have to head back to New Orleans tomorrow. But, there's something about this girl. About this night. The spark in her eyes, the way she laughs, and almost dares me with her experiences. I'm not going anywhere.

I move over to the sales associate, who is looking at me like she wouldn't mind seeing me naked.

"Is this all for you today, sir?" she asks.

I pull out my wallet and hand her my black American Express card. "This is all, thanks."

"Thank you for shopping with us, Mr. Pitz. Come back and see us soon." When she hands me my bag, her finger grazes the top of my hand.

This woman is pretty, but nothing compared to my angel in red, who is probably waiting for me in the lobby.

I nod and smile politely, then turn and rush back to meet my Vixen.

As I turn the corner, I spot her. My vixen. She really is the most beautiful woman I've ever seen, and it's a privilege to spend this time with her. I mean, seriously, how did I get so lucky? This gorgeous stranger rescued me from the most boring wedding I've ever been to and is taking me around her city during one of the most special times of the year. I'm slightly worried this is a dream.

She's removed one of her gloves so that she can take the tag off of the red earmuffs in her hand. There's a black and red plaid scarf draped over her arm too. There's a bag sitting by her feet, which I'm guessing holds socks because it's about the same size as my bag, which has my socks and gloves.

"Hey, did you get what you needed?" She nods toward the bag in my hand.

"Yep, I'm ready." I hold out my arm, gesturing for her to lead the way.

Once she puts the earmuffs on her head, which look abso-fucking-lutely adorable, she winds the scarf around her neck.

"We'd better get out of here or they might just lock us in for the night."

I shudder. "That would be my worst nightmare. Let's go."

"You don't like the idea of that, huh?" She giggles.

"Um, no, thank you. What if the mannequins come alive? Have you ever seen that movie? My mom used to put it on sometimes when I was little. Freaked me out."

"I can't say that I have seen that one. You're too funny." She pushes the door open, and we walk back out to the chilly night air. It stopped snowing a while ago, but it's still freezing.

"So how do we get to the rink?" I ask her.

"Well, it's a bit of a walk and time is ticking, so we'll just grab one of these rickshaws to Wolman Rink."

She leads us over to a rickshaw that looks like Christmas literally threw up on it. *All I Want for Christmas* by Mariah Carey is blasting from the small speaker the driver has attached to the back of his seat, facing the bench seat.

"Are you taking rides?" she asks the driver.

"Yes, I am. Where you headin'?" he asks her in a thick New York accent.

"Can you take us to Wolman Rink?" She steps onto the platform and sits on the bench seat.

"Yep, that'll be twenty." He turns and looks at me. "You gettin' in or what?"

"Right. Yes. Getting in." I hesitate, eyeing the wheels like they're about to file a complaint with OSHA. The frame creaks when I shift my weight forward. I mean, sure—I'm fit. I'm an NFL quarterback. But I'm also six-foot-two and two hundred fifteen pounds of solid muscle. Not exactly *rickshaw material.*

Still, I climb in—gingerly—half expecting the whole Christmas cart to collapse under me.

"Come on, Blitzen, don't be scared." She waves her hand toward her, motioning me to sit with her.

"I'm not scared as much as I don't want the tires to pop when

I get in." I chuckle, but lift myself up and into the seat next to her.

"Buddy, this ain't nothing. You in?" The driver's head is turned to the side, waiting for my answer.

"Yep, ready." Vixen places her hand on top of mine and curls her fingers under mine.

I look at her and wink. "This should be...fun."

She laughs. "Yes, it will be. We'll be at the rink in no time. Are you ready to have your mind blown with my ice skills?"

"One hundred percent ready for it. You aren't some professional figure skater or something, are you? You gonna embarrass me on the ice?" I let go of her hand and wrap my arm around her shoulder and pull her in closer to me.

Her head tilts from side to side. "Not exactly, but..."

"But..." I prod.

"I did play ice hockey from the time I was seven through college. I was a left wing." She lifts her shoulder and looks at me out of the corner of her eye.

"Wow, that's pretty amazing. So, you'll definitely embarrass me on the ice then. Awesome." I nod.

"You'll be fine. I'll hold your hand the whole time. I promise you, I won't let you fall." She whispers, leans in closer to me, then she places the softest kiss on my cheek.

I try to turn my head to meet her lips, but the rickshaw goes over a bump, leading us into the park, and she grabs on to the side.

"A little bumpy." She turns her head, but I can see the pink coloring her cheeks.

"So, Vixen—what's your favorite thing about Christmas?"

Her eyes soften, and for a second, the teasing slips away. "Hmm. I think it's that feeling you get walking outside when the air smells like snow, and everyone's pretending life's a little more magical than it really is."

"That's surprisingly deep for someone who just calls herself Vixen," I tease.

She shrugs. "I contain multitudes."

I grin. "For me, it's the food. My mom makes these ridiculous sugar cookies shaped like footballs. The frosting's terrible, but... it's kind of tradition."

"Football cookies. That tracks," she says, laughing. "Let me guess—you're one of those guys who turns Christmas dinner into a competitive sport?"

"Only if there's mashed potatoes involved."

"Good to know," she says, smiling.

I lean back and nod toward her. "Alright, your turn for a tougher one. Least favorite thing about Christmas?"

"Oh, easy." She lifts her gloved finger like she's making a dramatic declaration. "Those inflatable yard decorations. You know, the ones that collapse into sad plastic puddles during the day? Terrifying."

I laugh. "You're anti-inflatable? That's bold."

"They just... stare at you when they're half-deflated. Like Frosty's seen things."

"I feel like that's a personal story," I say.

"It might be," she says, mock-serious. "You?"

I think for a moment. "Gift wrapping. I cannot, for the life of me, fold corners properly. It always looks like I let a raccoon do it."

She laughs, head tipping back. "A big, strong guy like you taken down by Scotch tape. Tragic."

"It's humbling," I say. "I've learned to lean into the 'I tried' aesthetic."

She grins. "That's what bows are for. They distract from the chaos."

"Noted. I'll add bows next year. Maybe even a little glitter."

"Careful," she warns. "Glitter's a commitment. Once it's on you, it's forever."

I have a feeling I'll feel the same way about her when this night is over.

CHAPTER
FOUR

LIAM

Wollman Rink glows like a Norman Rockwell painting with its white ice, soft golden lights strung around the perimeter, and the dark silhouettes of the city rising behind the trees. The night is crisp, the kind of cold that nips at your nose but doesn't bite.

But none of it touches the heat that hits me when I look at her. She stands there in that red coat, cheeks flushed from skating and laughter, breath puffing in small clouds. The lights catch in her hair, turning her into something warm and bright against the winter night. And yeah... even if it were below freezing, that sight alone could thaw any man straight through.

She's skating circles around me, and it's not that it's hard to do since my skating skills are not top-tier. Sure, I can throw a football for seventy yards and work my way around three hundred pound linemen, but I cannot for the life of me find my balance on these skates. In my defense, the skates we rented aren't the best. The blades are dull and well past needing to be replaced. But I'm letting this little Vixen pull my ass around looking like an idiot.

"You're doing so good. I think you're ready to go on your own now, don't you?" She tries to let go of my hand, but I squeeze hers tighter.

"I'm not so sure I'm ready for that yet. You can't leave me." There might be a slight panic to my tone, but I don't even care. I brace my legs and stand stock still.

She belts out a laugh, dropping her head back. Once she catches her breath, she looks at me. "You got this. You're an athlete. I have faith in you, Blitzen."

"I don't know. I feel pretty unsteady—" What she just said stops me. "Wait. You know I'm an athlete?"

She opens her mouth, then closes it. Her gaze meets mine, and a slow smile forms on her lips. "I mean, you have all that," she gestures to my body. "Going on. And I can't even see the whole thing under the jacket."

"Uh huh." I slide myself closer to her and, with a confidence in my balance that I don't quite have, I reach out and slide my hand around her neck.

"And you don't look hot girl fit."

"What the hell is hot girl fit?"

"A body that looks good but lacks cardiovascular endurance." She lifts a brow. "Aesthetic only. No stamina."

I bark out a laugh. "Zero stamina? That's what you think of me?"

"I don't know," she says, pretending to inspect me like I'm a questionable produce item. "You *look* like you could run a mile, but you also give off strong 'needs an inhaler after climbing stairs' energy."

"Oh, that's rude." I tighten my hand at the back of her neck just enough to draw her a fraction closer. "Very rude, Vixen."

"Truthful," she counters, but her voice dips, betraying her.

"And what energy do *you* give off?" I ask.

She pretends to think. "Hot-girl fit with exceptional emotional intelligence."

I snort. "That's not a category."

"It is if I say it is."

"You realize," I say, leaning in until my forehead almost touches hers, "you're talking a lot of smack for someone who's currently one slip away from landing in my lap."

Her gaze flicks down—just for a second. "Please. If I wanted to be in your lap, I'd already be there."

My pulse stutters. "Is that right?"

She shrugs, all faux innocence. "I mean... you're the one holding my neck like you're about to make a move."

Oh, I am. Very much.

But before I can deliver a clever comeback—or actually act on the gravitational pull between us—her skate slips just a hair.

She grabs my jacket with both hands, eyes wide. "Okay, nope! Too close! Blitzen, stabilize me!"

I try, I really do.

But she's clutching me, and I'm overconfident, and suddenly we're both wobbling like newborn deer on ice.

"Don't fall," she warns.

"You're the one—"

She yelps, I overcorrect, and we end up chest-to-chest, her breath warm against my chin, our skates locked in a doomed tangle.

We freeze.

Her hands are fisted in my jacket.

My hand is still on her neck.

Her nose brushes mine. "If we fall," she whispers, "you're going down first."

"Gladly," I murmur, "but maybe not on the ice."

Her eyes flare just before she shoves me—playfully, barely—just enough to untangle our skates.

"Focus, athlete," she says, cheeks flushed. "We're here to skate, not flirt."

I grin. "Pretty sure we're doing both."

She groans, but she's smiling. "God help me, you might have the stamina after all." She shakes her head and looks away.

My hand falls, but I bend my head to try to catch her eye. "Come on, Vixen. Tell me what you really think of me. No bullshit."

"I'll tell you this." She purses her painted red lips and puts her hand on my shoulder. "I like your face. You have a sweet smile and an air of confidence that I'm into. Your eyes are mischievous, which should be a warning sign, but I find myself wanting to know more about you rather than walking away. You're fun to hang out with, and you follow along with me even when you don't know what my plans are. You roll with it, which tells me you're easygoing and able to adjust your plan when needed. So, I guess what I'm saying is, I'm pleasantly surprised by how my night turned out."

For a second, something warm hits me right in the chest.

Who the hell is this woman?

I've dated confidence before. I've met spontaneous. But I've never met someone who's both those things and somehow still impossible to predict. Someone who can make the entire room blur out just by looking at me like she means every damn word. It's... unnerving. And addictive.

A smile breaks across my face. "Okay, Vixen. I like you too. And I couldn't be happier with how my night turned out."

We're locked in a stare—one of those rare moments where everything goes quiet, and I swear something shifts. Right when I think she feels it too, *Jingle Bell Rock* blares through the speakers. She breaks eye contact, releases my hand, and pushes off, skating away from me backward with that smug little smirk.

The moment snaps in half. "Hey! You can't just leave me here on my own!" I shout over the music.

She lifts her chin and laughs—light, teasing, like I hadn't just handed her a piece of something real. "You got this, Blitzen. I believe in you! Come on, follow me!" She shouts back and waves her hand toward her.

And just like that, she turns my chest-tight, quietly emotional moment into a chase.

Damn her.

But I go after her anyway.

"I can't believe I'm doing this. I better not hurt myself or coach will have my ass." I mumble as I start to shuffle my feet.

"Just go for it! If you go too slow, you'll definitely fall. Slide and glide, my friend." She spins, then takes off at a speed that makes me a little nervous.

"Fuck. Okay, get yourself together, Pitz. You look like a pussy out here." My little pep talk is enough to get my glide on. One foot, then the other. *Okay, this isn't so bad. I think I can do this.*

"Look at you go! I knew you could do it." She spins around me again, then skates backward, watching me move.

"I don't understand how you can skate like that. Aren't you scared you're going to run into someone?" I'm kind of nervous about it, honestly. There's no way I can get to her safely if she gets hurt.

"You mean, like this?" She swerves and wiggles her hands in the air.

"Ha, ha funny girl." I'm trying to be serious, but I can't help but laugh. She looks so happy and carefree.

I stand here, just watching her. And it hits me—hard enough to knock the air out of my lungs.

Is it actually possible to fall for someone after only a few hours?

I used to give Archie so much shit for that—swearing he'd lost his mind when he and Emma clicked on day one.

But now… yeah. I get it.

And I don't want to get it.

Because I'm not that guy. I don't do commitment. I don't choose romance over football or my family or… anything, really. This night was supposed to be fun—one night, no expectations, no complicated aftermath.

Yet here I am, wanting things I shouldn't want.

Wanting to be in her space.

Wanting her in mine.

Wanting to know her—really know her, every sharp edge and soft part she hides behind the jokes.

It's ridiculous.

It's dangerous.

And if I were the kind of guy who let relationships matter, I already know exactly where I'd be headed with her.

Unfortunately, I'm not that guy.

So why does it suddenly feel like I could be?

Her long brown hair is flying behind her as she speeds around the rink. She keeps turning her head to find me, a smile on her face. And those eyes, glittering. She really is stunning.

And she looks like mine.

My feet are moving on their own accord now in her direction. I want to get to her and wrap her in my arms.

"You coming to get me, Blitzen?" She starts to giggle.

"I am." But I'm actually not, because I windmill my arms trying to keep my balance, but my feet slide out from under me. "Fuck!"

I land flat, not just on my ass, but completely laid out. I somehow manage not to hit my head on the ice, thankfully preventing a concussion.

"Holy shit, are you okay?" Ice sprays all over me as she comes to a stop next to me. When she bends down, she puts her hands on either side of my face. "You good?"

"I don't know," I whisper. "Maybe you should check my head."

"Did you bump it?" She slides her hands under my head, and I take the opportunity to take hold of her waist and pull her on top of me. "Oh! You little sneak. Are you hurt?" She braces one hand on the ice beside my head, the other on my chest, holding herself above me.

"I'm so hurt." I pout my lip and give her my best puppy dog look.

"Uh, huh. Where?" She's basically straddling me at this

point, in the middle of the rink. But I couldn't care less if people are watching us. Or worse, filming us.

"Here?" Her finger traces up my chest, and even through the fabric of my coat and suit, I can feel it. I've lost my voice, so I just shake my head and swallow.

"What about here?" She traces my lips with her gloved finger. The leather is smooth on my lips, but I want more.

Wrapping my hand around her wrist, I tug her in closer to me. "I think you should kiss it and make it better."

"You do, huh?" She's a breath away now. It wouldn't take much for our lips to meet.

The speakers crackle, and a calm, overly cheerful voice echoes across the rink. "Ladies and gentlemen, this is your last song of the skate session. Please finish your laps and exit the ice when the music ends."

"I guess that's our cue to leave," I say, brushing her lips with mine.

"Sounds like it." She sits up, straddling my hips, then swings one of her legs to meet the other so she's kneeling next to me. "Do you think you can get up on your own?"

"Probably not in a pretty way, but yeah, I'll manage." I'm slightly irritated that our moment was interrupted. Again. But I smile instead because I know that just because our time here is up, our night doesn't have to be over. "Hey, you getting hungry?"

I maneuver myself so I'm on all fours, which isn't a grateful look, but I just need to get on my feet so I can get to the side and pull my way back to the bench to remove these demon slicers.

"Starving." She holds out her hand to me as I manage to get up on my feet. "I know just the place."

CHAPTER
FIVE

LIAM

She's nibbling on her bottom lip as she looks at the menu. If New York hadn't already felt like some sort of Christmas caricature art, Serendipity feels like stepping into a daydream. It's a mix of retro kitsch, whimsical fantasy, and vintage charm. Pastel-pink walls, and Tiffany-style lamps hanging low over every table, and a collage of quirky antiques and old-fashioned clocks. It's as cute and quirky as the woman sitting across from me. But not nearly as sexy.

"So you said this place is known for its Frozen Hot Chocolate?" I ask her.

"Mmmhmm. It's so yummy. You have to try it." She sets her menu down and wiggles her eyebrows at me. "It's practically orgasmic."

"Orgasmic, you say?" I hold up my arm. "I'll take two, please!"

Her mouth drops open, entertained by my nonsense.

"Did you want one too?" I tease, smirking.

She clears her throat. "Why yes, I think I will."

The waiter comes by to take our order since he probably saw my raised arm. "Are you both ready to order?"

"Yes, I'll take the bacon mac and a frozen hot chocolate." She hands him her menu. "Oh, and can I also get a glass of water?"

He nods, then looks at me. "And you, sir?"

"I'll have a cheeseburger, hold the tomato, but can I get some extra pickles?" I look at him, and he nods. "Great, and I'll have a frozen hot chocolate too."

"I'll get that right in for you." He takes my menu and walks away.

"So...Vixen. Tell me about you. I know you're from New York and that you know my buddy, Aaron. How do you know him?" I ask.

Her earmuffs, which she had been wearing, are sitting in front of her on the table, and she takes them in her hands and starts to twist them back and forth. I can't tell if she's nervous or just needs to have something to do with her hands.

"I'm from New York City. I know Aaron because our families have been friends since we were babies. Or before that, really. Our dads went to college together and stayed in touch. Then when his family moved to New York, we spent a lot of time with them. He's like a brother to me." She looks up at me from under her long, dark lashes.

"Do you have any siblings?" I want to know everything about her.

"I have an older sister, and we're pretty close. She's just finishing up her sports medicine residency, so she'll be around more now."

"Where did you go to college?" I reach out my hand and take one of hers in mine.

"I just graduated from Boston College in May, and I'm back here now full-time. I'm considering getting my master's, but I'm not really sure I want to." She lifts a shoulder.

"Boston, huh? I haven't been there either. Do you like it better there or here?"

She leans across the table to get closer to me. "Don't tell anyone…" She puts her delicate finger on her lips. "I like Boston better."

I gasp. "You do? Wait, why would that be a secret?" I laugh.

She tilts her head back and forth. "You know…the rivalry between the Red Sox and the Yankees. Tale as old as time, my friend."

"Ahh…baseball. Gotcha."

"New York will always be my home though."

The waiter returns to the table with her water and two large bowls, each with what I assume is the frozen hot chocolate, topped with whipped cream. Definitely not on my food plan, but I'll indulge anyway. It looks amazing.

"Thank you," she says as he sets hers in front of her.

"Thanks, man." I look up and smile at him.

"My pleasure. Your food should be out shortly." He turns and walks to the table next to ours.

"What was your major in college?" I lift the straw from my drink, dragging the tip slowly across the whipped cream, and bring it to my mouth, letting a dollop cling to my lips. I glance up, and she's watching me—mouth slightly parted, eyes tracing the motion like she's memorizing it.

"Uh, what? What was the question?" She tucks a piece of hair behind her ear.

"Your major? What do you want to be when you grow up?" I chuckle.

"Excuse me, sir, but I'm very grown up." She winks at me, flirting again.

"Oh, I'm well aware of that." I laugh. "But what do you want to do with your degree?"

She takes a sip of her drink, sits back, and releases my hand. "Well, my degree is in business management. So managing… things." She looks off to the side, not meeting my eyes.

"That's cool. Do you have any jobs lined up yet, or are you already working?"

"I have a job, yes. I work in my family business, actually." She looks back at me with a smile.

"That's awesome. And lucky. What's your family business?" I take a drink of the most delicious concoction I think I've ever tasted. I'm not sure I can ever drink regular hot chocolate again after this.

"My family is in the sports business." She takes another sip of hers.

"You're kidding?" I sit back in my seat and set my hands on the table.

"Nope. I mean, we have other businesses too, but our parent company is sports related."

Makes sense—she's in the sports business, good friends with Aaron, and she was at the same wedding I attended. I could pry more, learn more about her—her name, where she works—but I'm not going to. Not tonight. This little game we're playing—trying to figure out if she knows who I am—is too much fun to ruin with facts.

Part of me would be disappointed if she does know. Ever since becoming a pro football player, I've been warned more than once to watch who I spend time with. Mainly women. It's a harsh reality that some people only want to get close because of your status. That's why I've stayed away from getting too close to any one woman. I hate that thought. Especially since I have friends who've found real, genuine relationships with amazing women.

As my agent reminds me often, they met their girls in college when they were still mildly famous. Now, apparently, I'm a "somebody," and I have to be careful.

But tonight, none of that matters. Tonight, not knowing who she really is—her name, her job, whether she even knows my name—is exactly what makes this dangerous little game addictive. It's just skating, just teasing, just laughter. No expectations. And for once, I can enjoy it without thinking about what comes next.

Before she can say more, the waiter brings our food to the table. He sets hers down in front of her first. Her mac and cheese is piled high with bacon chunks resting on top. It's bubbling over the sides and looks delicious. Then he sets my plate down in front of me. My burger sits on a big pink plate, with French fries taking over half the plate.

We both say thank you, and he leaves the table.

"Enough about me, tell me more about you, Blitzen. Where are you from?" She asks me.

I smile as I remove the tomato and the bottom part of the bun, setting them to the side on my plate. Then I put the lettuce on the top bun, and with my fork, place the burger patty on top. When I look up at her to answer, she's holding her fork but watching me.

"You a picky eater?" She smirks.

I laugh. "Ha, not really. I just try to limit my carbs, and I want a few fries, so I'll sacrifice half the bun."

"Ah, okay. So, your hometown?"

"Right, yes. Well, you know I'm from Kansas, but I live in New Orleans now for work. I have an older brother, and I was somewhat of a surprise to my parents, but I'm close with them. I still call my mom every day." I chuckle. "I'm a Sagittarius. Umm...what else? Oh, I went to college at Walker University, then transferred to Michigan for my last year, which you probably figured out since I know Aaron." I lift my brows and look at her.

She nods as she chews her food, then swallows. "Yes, I... figured that it was college."

"Yeah, it was my last year. If you don't already know, which I suspect you do because of the company we were in, I play football." I raise my brows, looking at her.

She nods and smiles. "Let's just keep it at that, okay? Don't tell me anything else about your career. I want to know the man under the helmet." She winks.

"You do, huh?" I chuckle. "Okay, sure. What else do you want to know?"

She purses her lips and puts her finger on her chin. "So you must have just had a birthday since you're a Sagittarius. Happy belated birthday." She lifts her water to me in cheers. "Um, were you happy or sad to leave Walker and go to Michigan?"

"Yes, it was on December 10th, and thank you. As for my transfer, it was the hardest decision I've had to make so far, honestly. My friends at Walker are like family to me. Don't get me wrong, I have some good buddies from Michigan. I mean, I wouldn't be here if I didn't care about them, but it's just different." I shrug.

"I get that. I don't have a ton of close friends, but my sister and I are really close, and like I said, Aaron is like a brother. It was hard being away from them when I was at college."

Even though she has said it twice now that they're like family, I have to know if it's ever been something more. "Have you and Aaron ever dated?"

Her head drops back, and she lets out a deep belly laugh. "Oh god, no. It's never been like that between us."

"Okay, good to know. I just want to make sure that me being here with you won't cause any problems if y'all are close, close."

"Ew, no. I mean, he's a great guy, but I have never seen him as anything more than a friend." She takes another bite of her food.

"But you don't have a boyfriend, do you?"

"Blitzen, I wouldn't be here with you if I did." She gives me a flirty smile. "You don't have a girlfriend, do you?"

I shake my head. "No, I don't have a girlfriend." I'm not gonna close down an opportunity with this girl by explaining that my job is a priority right now, because if I have a chance with her, even for one night, I'm not blowing it.

"Good. I'm glad to hear it." We stare at each other, smiling.

"Are you ready to move to our next adventure?"

"Vixen, I'll go anywhere with you." I reach for her hand again, and she places hers in mine.

CHAPTER
SIX

LIAM

We walk out of the restaurant, and she slips her gloves back on, smoothing the leather over each finger with slow, precise movements that feel far more intimate than they should. I leave mine off—the cold feels good on my hands—and she reaches for one without hesitation. Her leather-covered fingers lace through mine as she makes a right onto 60th Street, tugging me along like she already knows where she wants us to go.

I should feel ridiculous walking beside her in an all-white suit, like I was about to headline a Vegas magic show or pose for a boy-band comeback album. But I don't. Maybe it's because she keeps looking at me like I'm something worth looking at. Or maybe it's the heat simmering under my skin just from being near her.

We walk another block, the city humming around us, before curiosity gets the better of me. Or maybe the tension does— thick, steady, impossible to ignore.

"So," I say, "be straight with me. Why the red?"

She laughs—low, warm, the kind of sound that strokes

against my skin without ever touching me. "Since Aaron invited me at the last minute," she continues, "he forgot to mention the dress code. I didn't know it was an all-white wedding until we were already walking in. All red was what I had."

"It's a bold choice."

"I'm an old-school kind of girl." She lifts one shoulder in a slow, confident shrug. "If I'm going to stand out, I'm going to commit. That said, I'm bold, but I didn't love taking attention from the bride. That wasn't the intention."

It's the first time tonight she sounds even slightly unsure. It makes her seem more real. And somehow, more dangerous.

"Is the 'fish-out-of-water' outfit the real reason you wanted to leave the wedding? Because you in that red coat against a terrace full of white felt like... fireworks waiting to happen."

"Partly," she adds, her pace slowing as her gloved fingers tighten around mine, "more than that... I wanted to leave with you."

The words land somewhere low and warm in my chest. "Why me?"

She gives me a long, deliberate look—slow, lingering, like she's memorizing me. "Well... it might have something to do with you showing up dressed like—" She gestures at me with a lazy flick of her leather-clad fingers. "—a very charming marshmallow."

I groan. "Terrific. Exactly the look I was going for."

"A *handsome* marshmallow," she corrects, stepping just a bit closer. "The kind you don't toss in cocoa. The kind you... savor."

Her tone dips on the last word, and I feel the pull of it low in my stomach.

"This?" I ask, my voice rougher than it should be.

She nods. "I wanted to walk through Manhattan at Christmas time with the handsome stranger who made me forget my senses for a few hours." Her breath brushes the air between us, warm and close. "And maybe... a few hours more."

She steps just close enough that the side of her body glances against mine, her coat brushing my suit. It's nothing overt. Just enough to make my pulse thicken. Just enough to make me imagine her without the coat, without the gloves, without the distance.

"Where are we going next?" I look down at her as she looks up at me.

"We're heading back toward Central Park. I thought we could take a carriage ride. Have you ever been on one?"

"I've ridden a horse before, but never in a carriage." I bring her gloved hand up to my lips and kiss the back of her hand. "Hey," I stop walking and face her. "Thank you for doing all this with me tonight. It's seriously the most fun I think I've ever had."

"Really?" She smiles and tilts her head.

I nod. "I swear."

"I'm glad. I'm having a good time too." She turns, and we continue walking.

We continue walking and can hear another street musician somewhere nearby playing Christmas carols. There's a comfortable silence between us as we walk.

Right before we cross the street to the park, we see a vendor selling various Christmas trees, some decorations, and a display stand with ornaments hanging from it.

"Hang on a sec. Let's look and see what they have. You should definitely get something to remember this night in Manhattan, right?" She looks up at me, and the reflection of the lights in her eyes makes them sparkle.

"For sure, but I think you should too. I don't want you to forget my handsome face." I wink at her.

"Oh, there's no way I'd forget your face, or this night." She takes an apple ornament off the hanger and turns toward me. "I'm really glad we were both cold and bored."

"Me too, Vixen. Me. Too." I take her other hand in mine and pull her in closer to me. "Have I told you how beautiful you are?"

"Tell me." She breathes.

I slide my hand into her hair and step in closer still. "You're beautiful in a way that blindsides a guy. Not just because of your face—though that alone could ruin me—but because you're vibrant and unpredictable, like the whole season wrapped into one woman. You've got that Christmas kind of magic... the kind that pulls you in, warms you up, and makes you want more. It's the kind of beauty a man doesn't forget."

"Hey. You gonna buy that, lady?" The vendor interrupts us.

Still holding my gaze, she answers him, but pulls away from my hold. "Yep. I'll take this one and this one." She holds out an ornament of the Rockefeller tree.

"Which one is mine?" I point to her hand.

"The apple is yours. The tree is mine, because that's the first time I noticed the green in your eyes, and they shimmered in the light of the tree, and I didn't want to look away."

Her teeth graze her lip. "And I get the apple because you're _"

"Bold, bright and impossible to ignore."

She lifts a shoulder. "I was thinking because you're too tempting not to want to take a bite out of."

I let out a groan, and she smiles, then ducks her head and walks over to the vendor.

"That'll be thirty." The guy says.

"I'll get it." I walk over and pull out forty bucks.

"Oh, wait, one more thing." She grabs a Santa hat off another stand.

"Twenty," the vendor says.

"Twenty? You've got to be kidding me?" She puts her hands on her hips and huffs.

"I got it. Here you go, buddy." I hand him another twenty. "Keep the change. Merry Christmas." I nod, then reach for her hand. "Let's go, my little Vixen."

As we walk, she starts to laugh. "You just got ripped off. We could have gotten that same hat at Duane Reade for half that price."

"Ah, who cares. And you picked it up, not me!" I wrap my arm around her waist and tickle her side.

She giggles and squirms away from me. "No tickling!"

"Okay, let's go find this carriage." I wrap my arm around her again, and we continue to walk.

"Oh! There's one!" She points to an all-black carriage with a red seat bench and a gorgeous black horse. There are white lights attached to the carriage and along the harness. We walk over to it, and she asks the driver, "Are you taking rides?"

"I sure am, hop on in." He waves his arm toward the carriage with a wide smile. "I'm Frank, and I'll be your driver tonight. Hey, don't I know you?" He looks at me.

I don't really want to be rude, but I also don't want to be talking about football the whole time with the driver, so I just smile and wink at him. "Thanks for the ride."

I guide her over to the step and hold her hand as she steps up. "My lady."

"Thank you," she says, then places a kiss on my cheek. I can feel the heat from her lips even after she pulls away.

Once she takes a seat, I climb up and settle beside her. I drape my arm along the back of the bench, hand resting on her shoulder, and pull her a little closer, letting her lean into me. I think I hear a quiet sigh, but it could just be the horse's hooves clopping over the pavement. Either way, it hits me—I love having this woman in my arms.

Her warmth presses against me, soft and solid at the same time, and the faint scent of her wraps around me. My chest tightens in that way that makes me want to hold her closer, to feel her even more. Everything else—the cold, the noise, the moving horse—blurs into the background. Frank rattles off the route he's taking around the park, but I barely register the words.

All I can focus on is her—the way she fits perfectly against me, the subtle weight of her body pressed into mine, the heat of her skin against my arm. My pulse jumps every time she shifts just enough to brush against me, and a low, dangerous thought slides through my head: I don't want to let go, not now, not ever.

After we're on our way, and Frank leaves us to ourselves, I tug her to me and place a hand on her leg. "Are you cold?" I press my lips on the top of her head.

"A little, but you're keeping me warm." She leans her head back to look at me.

"Can I tell you something?" I ask, looking between her eyes and her lips.

"Yes," she breathes.

"I've never wanted to kiss someone as badly as I want to kiss you." I inch my face closer to hers.

She reaches her hand up to my face. "So then kiss me." Her hand holds the back of my neck, and she pulls me toward her even closer.

I don't care that Frank is with us, or that people passing by can see us. I *need* to taste these cherry red lips. "Are you sure?"

"If you don't kiss me, Blitzen, I'm going to kiss you—"

Before she can finish what she's saying, I press my lips to hers. Her mouth is soft, warm, and impossibly sweet, and I want more than just a taste—I want all of her. I trace the seam of her lips with my tongue, and when she parts, I slide inside, feeling her tongue brush against mine like velvet. She tastes like a danger I want to keep indulging.

She twists against me, hips shifting in my lap without breaking the kiss, and I lift her legs, draping them over mine. Her body molds against mine, every curve pressing into me, every movement setting a fire in my chest. My hand slides along her thigh, cupping her ass cheek through the layers, feeling the heat radiating through her clothes. I want her closer, pressed fully against me, skin to skin, but even this—layers and all—is enough to make me ache.

Her hand snakes up the back of my head, tangling in my hair, pulling me deeper. Our tongues slide and tangle together in a slow, hungry rhythm. I feel her pulse in the subtle pressure of her hands, her hips shifting, the faint tremor in her body against mine. Every touch sparks something low and dangerous in me, a tension that makes my hands clench and my pulse pound.

Time ceases. Frank rattles off directions somewhere behind us, but I don't hear a word. I don't care. All that exists is her, the way she presses into me, and the ache of wanting more.

Finally, I pull back slightly, resting my forehead against hers. My chest rises with the burn of desire, hands still lingering on her body, reluctant to leave. "Come back to my hotel with me," I say, voice low, certain, a command disguised as a promise.

She pulls back and looks around, then back at me and nods. "Okay." Then she slams her mouth on mine again.

We kiss until my lips feel swollen, but I don't want to stop. I never want to stop.

A throat clears. "Hate to interrupt you lovebirds, but we're almost back to our departure area."

I pull away from our kiss and turn toward Frank. "Actually, can you drop us off in front of The Plaza?"

"No problem, sir." He nods his head.

I look back at her, and she's biting her lip, watching me, but she has a soft smile on her lips. I take my thumb and press it against her lip and tug it free from her teeth. "That's mine to bite."

She touches her tongue to the tip of my thumb. "Fuck. Yes." I groan.

The carriage pulls to a stop, and Frank steps out of his seat and waits for us to disembark. I step off first, then turn and reach for her, grabbing hold of her waist and lifting her off the carriage. When I set her down, I get into my pocket for my wallet and hand Frank three hundred dollar bills and shake his hand.

"Sir, I'm so sorry to ask, but can I get your autograph?" Frank leans in.

I glance at him, heart skipping a beat. Shit. Keep it calm. Keep it casual. "Yeah, sure. Do you have something for me to sign?" I pat my pockets. "I don't have anything on me."

He pulls out a notepad and a pen from a pocket in his coat and hands them both to me. "I really appreciate it. My grandson, Michael, is a fan. He won't believe it when I tell him I had you in my carriage tonight."

I take the notepad and lean slightly away from her, keeping my voice low. Scribbling quickly, I sign my name and add a little note to Michael. My fingers brush the pen, the movement deliberate but quiet.

She leans over to watch, curiosity written all over her face. "What was that about?" she asks softly, tilting her head.

I slide the notepad back to Frank without looking at her and keep my tone casual, almost teasing. "Just a little fan moment," I murmur, letting the mystery hang.

Frank smiles wide, eyes sparkling behind his glasses. "Thank you, Mr. Pitz. Michael will be thrilled."

I nod, slipping the moment away from her notice, and turn back to the bench, letting her wonder what exactly just happened.

Her lips twitch with a smile, but she doesn't press. I let my arm stay draped around her shoulders, feeling her warmth against me, her subtle shiver under my touch.

She looks up and smiles. "Come on, Blitzen. I'm cold and ready for you to warm me up." She takes my hand in hers and we walk into The Plaza together, hand in hand.

CHAPTER
SEVEN

LIAM

As soon as we get into the elevator to go up to my floor, I put my hands on her hips and gently push her to the wall. "I can't wait to get my hands on you." I probably sound desperate, but I am, so I don't give a fuck.

"Me too. I can't wait to see what's under this coat." She grabs the lapel of my jacket and tugs.

I bend down and kiss her, slow and deep.

The elevator doors open, and she breaks the kiss and looks to the exit. "This is us?"

I look at the room numbers on the elevator sign and nod. "Yep, this is us."

She doesn't wait for me, she just walks out and then stops and spins around to face me. "What's your room number?"

"Twelve fifty five." I point to the left. "This way."

She starts to walk down the hall toward my room, but I swoop in behind her and pick her up and carry her the rest of the way in my arms.

"What are you doing?" She laughs.

"I can't wait. I want you in my room as soon as possible." I move quickly down the hallway.

She leans in and starts kissing and sucking on my neck, making me groan.

When I get to my door, I set her on the ground, and I pull out my key card and tap it. Once it clicks, I push it open and hold the door for her to enter.

As soon as the door closes, I'm on her. I step up behind her and move her hair to the side, dropping kisses on her neck up to the soft spot behind her ear while we walk toward the bed. "You smell so good. Like fresh roses."

She turns in my arms when we get to the bed. She pulls off her gloves one by one as I start to unbutton my coat. I set it on one of the chairs at the foot of the bed, and take her gloves from her hand and set them with my jacket. I reach for her buttons on her coat, and we lock eyes.

Her smile is wicked when she reaches for my suit jacket. I'm unbuttoning her coat while she unbuttons my jacket and pushes it off my shoulders. When I get to her bottom button, she wiggles her arms free and drops her coat on the floor.

She kept her coat on even in the restaurant, and now I know why. The top of her outfit is sleeveless and hugs her tits just right, then straight down her body, pants flaring just below her calves. I never knew pants could be so sexy. And it's all red. Like the color of her lipstick.

I make quick work of my shirt and tie, then I kick off my shoes.

She takes a seat in one of the chairs to remove her shoes, but I kneel in front of her. "Let me."

"Okay," she says, leaning back in the seat.

Fuck me, even her feet are perfect. I remove both of her heels, then lift one of her legs and kiss her ankle. I set her foot back down on the floor and stand. I reach for her hands and pull her up from the chair.

She turns and faces the bed, and sweeps her hair over her shoulder, giving me access to the back zipper. "Unzip me?"

"Fuck, yes." I'm so jacked up, I fumble with the small zipper for a minute until I get a good grip, then I practically rip it off while I make my way down her back. As the zipper parts, I see a red lacy bra, and lower I see a red lacy thong to match. When the zipper reaches the end, she reaches around to the back and unfastens her bra, and it drops to the ground.

Am I holding my breath? I think I might be because I feel like I'm about to pass out from anticipation.

When she turns, I see the most perfect pink nipples. I reach for her, just as she grabs the button on my pants. "You're so fucking beautiful, Vixen. How did I get so lucky to spend the night with you?"

"You're not too bad yourself. Your body is insane. The abs... Jesus H. I can't wait to run my tongue over them."

She pushes my pants down my legs, and I step out of them. We face each other and can't hold back any longer. Our mouths collide, and I grab the backs of her thighs and lift her, so her pussy fits directly over my hard on in my boxers.

I walk to the side of the bed and lay her down without breaking our kiss. I drift a hand to the top of her thigh and make my way to her center. She's soaked through the lace, and I push it aside and run my index finger through her wetness. I pull back and look into her eyes. "This is all mine."

"Yes," she moans. "Yours."

I kiss her lips again, but don't deepen it. I bend down and kneel on the floor, grabbing the tiny strings of her thong and pulling it down her legs, revealing the most perfect pussy I've ever seen. It's perfectly pink, just like her nipples, with a thin stip of trimmed hair, and she's glistening. For me.

I drape one of her legs over my shoulder, and grab under her thigh and spread her open to me. I can't wait another second to taste her, so I bend my head and run my tongue from her hole to her clit. She's just as sweet as I thought she would be, and I feel like I'll never get enough of her. I could actually die between her legs and be thankful she allowed me to.

I lean in, unable to hold myself back any longer, and press my mouth where she wants me most.

The sound she makes—low, broken, helpless—nearly undoes me. It shoots straight through my chest, straight through every place I've ever tried to keep under control. I grip her thigh harder, anchoring her to me, because for a second I'm not sure I can stay steady under the force of wanting her.

She tastes like heat and surrender and something dangerously close to addiction.

I don't even try to slow down. I can't. Not when she arches into me, not when her breath comes in uneven little gasps, not when she keeps whispering my name like it's been pulled from somewhere deep inside her.

Every sound, every shiver, every press of her hips feels like it brands itself into me.

I tighten my hold on her, pulling her closer, sinking into her completely.

And the way she responds—God—

It's enough to make me forget every line I swore I wouldn't cross.

"Oh, God, that feels so good." She takes my head in both of her hands, holding me to her as I lick, suck, and devour her pussy.

I move my hand from her leg and push my middle finger into her, thrusting it in and out as I flick her clit with my tongue. Her hands fall from my head, but I see her grip the comforter by her sides. And when I look up her body, her back is slightly arched and her head tilted, eyes closed, mouth open, panting. She looks like a goddess.

When I start to feel her pulse around my finger, I suck harder on her clit and move my hand faster, creating more friction as she comes.

"Yes, just like that," she moans. "Don't stop."

As if I could. I want to taste her come on my tongue, and I want to lick up every drop.

When she starts to come, she tries to close her legs, but I don't let her. I hold both legs in place as she rides it out. "Oh my god. Fuck. Feels. So. Good."

I'm so focused on her pleasure that I don't even realize my own orgasm building. I mean *fuck*, my hand isn't even on my dick, and I blow. Just from making her come.

When she starts to come down, her body relaxes, and I release her legs, climbing up her body, kissing every inch along the way. "You're so fucking perfect. And the way you look when you come had me coming all over the carpet."

I kiss her on the lips and then slide my tongue into her mouth. She moans when my tongue reaches hers, no doubt tasting herself on my tongue.

"I need you inside me. Like right now." Her hands reach around my back, and she runs her hands up and down, stopping at the top of my ass. "Fuck me, Blitzen." She tilts her hips, trying to angle herself so the head of my cock is at her entrance.

I pull back just enough that when she moves her hips again, my dick pushes inside of her. We both moan this time. I thrust in a little deeper, then deeper again, until I'm completely sheathed by her pussy. "You're so fucking tight. Am I hurting you?"

She shakes her head. "Don't you dare stop."

"Not a chance." I start fucking her, slow at first, then both of us begin to lose control, and our rhythm gets a little sloppy as we edge near our orgasms.

"Look at me," I murmur.

Her lashes lift, just barely, but enough.

One glance and I'm gone.

She looks wrecked in the most stunning way. Her hair spilled across the pillow, her skin flushed, her breath catching every time I move even slightly. I've never wanted anything more in my life than to keep her right here, trembling.

Her fingers tug at my hair again. A deeper sound breaks from her throat, soft but desperate, and I feel the answering pull low inside me, tightening everything.

I move my mouth against hers again. Slow, deliberate, claiming her inch by inch. Not explicit. Just undeniable.

Her whole body responds, arching, tightening, her toes curling against my back. I hold her steady, not letting her escape the intensity building between us, not letting myself escape it either.

She says my name again…shaky, breathless.

I've never wanted to hear anything more.

Her hand slides down from my hair to my cheek, thumb brushing my skin. A gentle touch, but somehow more devastating. There's trust in it—so much quiet, unspoken trust that it nearly undoes me.

I lift my head for a fraction of a second, just long enough to kiss the inside of her wrist—slow, reverent, a promise more than a touch. She shivers violently, grabbing the pillow with her free hand, breath hitching like she wasn't prepared for tenderness in the middle of all this heat.

"Don't stop," she whispers, and there's something raw in it. Something honest. Something that pulls me closer, deeper.

"Come for me. Strangle my cock, baby. I can't hold it much longer." I drive into her faster and faster, as she presses her nails into my back. And fuck me, is that a turn on.

"Yes," she pants. "Fuck me harder. I'm so close."

I reach down between us and rub her clit in circles, because I'm gonna blow any second, and I'm a firm believer that a lady comes first. "You close? I can't hold it much longer."

She nods. "Kiss me."

I tilt my head and kiss her deeply, my tongue twirling around hers. When she wraps her lips around my tongue and she sucks, I can't hold back any longer. My balls start to tingle, so I rub her clit faster, trying to get her there with me.

When she breaks the kiss and cries out, I feel her pulsing around my cock, as I explode into her.

I rest my forehead on the bed next to her head as we catch our breath. "Fuck me, that was hot," I say breathily.

"So hot," she breathes. "When can we do it again?" She turns her face to mine and we both smile.

"Give me five." I place a kiss on her shoulder and then pull out of her and lie on my side facing her.

She sits and then turns to me. "Be right back." Then she walks into the bathroom.

While she's in there, it hits me. I didn't wear a fucking condom. *Fuck.* I've never not worn a condom. Shit.

I move up the bed and lean against the headboard as I wait for her to come out. I don't bother to cover up because I do intend to get inside her again as soon as possible. And I really don't want her to cover up either.

She walks out of the bathroom with pink in her cheeks and a satisfied smile. That I put there. When she reaches the bed, I pat the spot next to me. But instead of sitting next to me, she climbs on top of me and straddles my waist. My dick is pretty happy about it and decides he doesn't need five minutes after all.

Her hands rest on my chest, and she leans down to kiss me. As the kiss deepens, she starts rubbing her bare pussy up and down my hardened cock.

I grip her waist and pull back enough to speak. "Baby, as much as I love this, um, we didn't use a condom."

She stops moving and sits up. "Oh shit. Right."

"I'm clean!" I blurt out. "I've never had sex without a condom."

"Okay, good. I'm clean too. I'm sorry, I just got lost in the moment, I guess. I'm on the pill too, so we're good."

I nod. "So yeah, then we should be okay." I'm not sure who I'm trying to convince, but my dick is winning the battle.

CHAPTER
EIGHT

LIAM

My dick might be broken. After three rounds of being buried deep inside the prettiest pussy I've ever seen, and a top-notch blow job that left traces of her red lipstick on my cock, we both fell asleep.

She's lying on my chest right now, and my arm is wrapped around her, holding her to me. I've never actually slept with someone like this. I don't really like to be touched when I'm sleeping. It makes me too hot. But with her, I could get used to this.

Her hair fans out across my shoulder and onto the pillow. It looks and feels like silk, and against her creamy skin, she looks a little like snow white, but with long hair.

Thing is, though, I'm not ready to say goodbye to her. I've never felt like this about anyone. Ever. I wouldn't say I'm a player. Okay, maybe I am a little, but I've never had a girl that's made me want...more.

I'm not sure anything can come of it with me living in New

Orleans and her here, but my season is almost over, and a lot of the guys have houses in different places in the off-season. And I'll have time to travel, so maybe I should take a shot.

I kiss her head and start to stroke her back. "You awake?"

She hums. "I am now." Her hand on my chest starts to drift toward my growing dick.

"Keep touching me like that and I'm gonna start thinking I made Santa's damn naughty list."

I pause a beat and grin. "And honestly? Feels worth it."

As much as I want to bury myself inside her right now, I want her to know that last night was special. And I kind of want to see where her head is. I don't want to embarrass myself by going for something that doesn't have a chance.

"Yeah? I kinda like you, so I guess we both win." She's kissing my chest, and her hand snakes under the covers, and she takes my cock in her hand, and starts stroking it.

I groan. "That feels so fucking good. You keep that up and I'll forget what I wanted to say."

She looks up at me. "Oh, sorry. Did you want to say something? This is the part where we say goodbye and thanks for the memories?" She laughs, but it's forced.

I kiss her to stop her from thinking the worst. "I'm not ready to say goodbye. That's actually what I wanted to tell you. But I don't want to freak you out." I take hold of her waist and pull her up so she's straddling me.

She sits up and, in one of the sexiest moves I've ever seen, she twists her hair and works it into a knot at the top of her head. Seriously, why is that so sexy?

"You won't freak me out. What's up?" She places her hands on my chest.

"Well, I just wanted to say thank you again for the most amazing night. I've never met anyone like you, who I felt so comfortable with right away. Like completely drawn to you." I run my hands over the top of her thighs. "Is that cheesy?"

She bites her bottom lip and smiles. "Cheesy? No, not at all. I like it. And I like you." She sucks in a breath. "I had a great night with you too. It was unexpected, but that's kind of the best part, right?" She tilts her head to the side and lifts a brow. "You, Blitzen, were a very nice surprise." She bends down and kisses me on the lips.

I wrap my hand around her neck and deepen the kiss. We break apart, panting. "So I'm not the only one thinking we had a connection?"

"No, it's not just you. I feel it too. But I'll be honest with you. This isn't something I was looking for, and I'm not really sure what we can do about it since we don't live near each other. Do you have any ideas?"

"Well, I might. I mean, if you want to see if the magic goes beyond Christmas, I would love to see you again."

She sits up again and traces the muscles on my chest and down to my stomach. "I would love to see you again too."

"Good." We smile at each other.

"So, your idea?" She prompts.

"One of my best friends and his fiancée did long distance while she finished school. I mean, we could try it and see how it goes." I really want her to say yes.

"Hmm...I'm not opposed to trying it. Maybe we keep it light until we spend more time together and see how it all works out? No pressure." She takes my hands in hers.

"Right, no pressure. We see where it goes." I smile. "I have to warn you though, I have no idea what I'm doing. I've never tried to have a relationship. But, most of my close friends are all hooked up, so I think they're good examples." I laugh. "That probably sounds stupid."

"Not at all. Tell me about them." She rolls off of me and lies on her side next to me.

I turn toward her so I can look at her. "What do you want to know?"

"I don't know. Just tell me about them. You've talked about

them a few times, so I assume they're important to you. So if we're going to try this on for size, I should probably know about the people in your life." She props her head on her hand.

"Well, they're my favorite people in the world, so I could probably talk about them all day," I smirk. "The three I'm closest to are Beck, Casey and Archie. We all played together at Walker and were roommates. Beck and Casey's twin sister, Charlie, are getting married this spring. Casey and his girl, Noelle, finally got their shit together last year. They were best friends, but we all knew it was something more."

"Oh, I love that." She smiles. "The way you talk about them…your face lights up."

"Yeah, I love these guys. Archie is my best friend. He and his wife, Emma, are the ones I spend the most time with. They have a little girl, Lainey, who is the cutest thing ever." I tuck a stray strand of hair behind her ear.

"Are they around our age?" She runs her hand up and down my arm.

"Yep. Archie and I are the same age, and I guess Emma is too, actually. Funny story… they hooked up one night at a party, and she got knocked up. It was a whole thing because she was on scholarship for golf, and Arch was entering the draft after the season, so it wasn't ideal timing. I still can't imagine being a dad right now. It's wild to me. I mean, don't get me wrong, he's the best dad, but the thought of having a kid right now…" I shiver.

"Do you not want kids?" She asks.

"Oh no, I absolutely do, just not any time soon. My schedule is crazy, and when I have kids, I want to make sure I'm present for them if that makes sense?" I raise a brow.

"Yeah, it makes total sense." She nods.

"Archie is lucky because he plays near his hometown, so they have a lot of help from his parents, and her parents also moved there too. So it works for them. I'm sure you know who he is. He's kinda hard not to know. He's got a loud personality." I chuckle thinking of him.

"I might know who he is." She smirks. "But I don't know him personally. He seems like a fun guy though."

"He is. And he's the same in person as you see on TV. One of the best guys I know."

"I'm happy you have friendships like that. They're hard to come by. I only have a few close friends, too, but my sister is my best friend. Speaking of...I have to meet her for lunch today. What time is it anyway?" She turns and looks for her phone.

It's not on the nightstand beside us, and I have no idea where mine is. She gets out of bed and pulls out her phone from her coat pocket.

"Oh shit! I have 14 missed calls between my sister and Aaron. I probably should have said goodbye to him last night when we left. He likely called my sister looking for me." She lifts her phone to her ear.

"Do you need to go now?" I sit up and turn my body to the side of the bed.

"Uh, yeah, I should get going soon. It's almost ten. I need to go home and change. Should probably shower too." She sets her phone down and gives me a wicked smile.

I walk toward her and wrap my arms around her waist, and lift her in my arms. "How about we shower together?"

"I don't think I have time for that, but...I could be persuaded to fuck you again."

"Persuaded, huh?" I bark out a laugh. "I accept that challenge." I walk us back to the bed and lay her down, then brace my weight on my arm as I climb over her and settle between her parted legs.

"You better make quick work of it though. I gotta go, Blitzen." Our faces are practically touching, and she wraps her arms over my shoulders and closes the distance with a kiss.

I suck her bottom lip into my mouth, and she moans. Then I make my way to her neck and down to her breasts. My hips start to rock on their own accord right through her pussy, as I suck one of her nipples into my mouth. The crown of my thickening cock rubs against her clit, and she grabs my hair and tugs my head, forcing me to look at her.

"If you don't put that gorgeous dick inside me, you're going on the naughty list." She tilts her hips, trying to put me inside of her.

"But I've been a very good boy this year." I drop my mouth to hers, and slip my tongue inside of hers, just as I thrust into her, making her moan into my mouth.

Our pace turns frantic as our hips grind against each other. My open mouth is hovering over hers, our breaths becoming more rapid with every stroke. "Don't come until I say. I'm nowhere near ready to be done with this pussy." I touch the tip of my tongue to hers. "I can't get deep enough." Even to my own ears, I sound more in control than I actually feel. "I want to fuck you so hard that you'll be thinking about me for days."

"Yes, please," she pants.

To tease her and to hold off my own orgasm, I slow my pace and pull out completely, then rub my cock against her clit. Once. Twice. "Do you feel what you do to me?" I slam back into her pussy hard to the hilt. "You drive me crazy." *Kiss.* "Make me feel like I've lost control." *Kiss.* "I'm not ready to leave you. Want to stay inside you."

"Harder. Fuck me harder." Her hands slide down my back, and she takes hold of my ass, squeezing. She might even leave a bruise. *I hope she does.*

"Goddamn, you feel so good. Made for me." My pace quickens because my dick is fully in charge now, chasing euphoria.

"Oh god, I'm gonna come. Liam!" she cries out.

It's not lost on me that she just said my name, but I'm not gonna ruin the moment by calling her out on it. "Come, baby. I'm gonna leave my mark on you, so I need you to get there." I reach between us and circle her clit with two fingers.

We're both becoming so frantic, and I really don't want to blow before she does. I lean down and take her mouth in a searing, wet kiss. It's hot and dirty, and just what she needs to push her over the edge. I feel her pussy start to strangle my dick. "That's it. Come for me." I kiss her through her peak, then I pull out just as my orgasm hits.

I push up on my arm and take my cock in my other hand, pumping as hot ropes of cum shoot out onto her stomach. "Fuck me, is that hot."

She releases my ass and brings her hands to her belly and starts to *fucking trace* her fingers through my cum, spreading it around and up to her breasts, circling her nipples. Then she reaches down to her belly button, where some more of my cum has pooled, and she swipes her finger through it and brings it to her lips and sucks it into her mouth.

"Holy fucking shit. You might make me erupt again just seeing you suck my cum off your finger." I pull on my cock one more time, squeezing every last drop onto her. "You truly are meant for me. I'm one hundred percent convinced. I can't ever let you go now."

I shift my weight and lie down by her side. She's still tracing my cum on her body, so I cover one hand with mine and follow her pattern, rubbing it into her skin. Branding her. Marking her as mine.

She looks at my face and gives me a satisfied smile. "I feel like jelly now. I'm not sure I can actually move to leave."

I lean over and kiss her softly. "You're so beautiful. Let me go get you a washcloth to clean my mess off of you." Even though I don't want to. "You can still join me for a quick shower, you know?" I wiggle my brows at her.

She laughs. "If I get in the shower with you, there's no way I'll make it to lunch on time. I still need to go home, remember. I can't show up in last night's clothes."

I kiss her one more time, then get off the bed. Walking to the end of the mattress, I grab my pants, fish out my phone, and see that I also have some texts from our group chat, including one from Archie. And one from Sabine. I reply to everyone but her. I'm not wasting time with my Vixen right now.

I set the phone down on the table between the two chairs at the end of the bed. "Be right back." I walk into the bathroom and get a washcloth and wet it.

When I get back to the room, she's sitting up against the headboard, watching me, smiling. Her hair has fallen out of her bun, and her cheeks are slightly pink. And she looks thoroughly fucked. Goddamn if that doesn't make me proud.

I sit on the edge of the mattress and wipe my cum off her stomach and move up to her breasts. "You look so pretty painted in my cum. I hate to wash it off."

She starts to laugh. "Yeah, but it'll dry soon, and no one likes that. Might be a little uncomfortable on my way home too." She winks at me.

I finish cleaning her off and then fold the washcloth and set it near the foot of the bed. "Are you gonna tell me your name before you leave? If we're planning to see where this goes, I can't call you Vixen forever." I take her hand in mine.

"Hmm...I guess you're right. Besides, it's not really fair, is it, since I know your name." She puts her finger on her chin.

"Exactly." I lift our hands and kiss the back of hers.

"Alie. My name is Alie." She leans forward closer to me.

"Alie. That's pretty." I meet her in a quick kiss, then pull back. "I better get in the shower or I might miss my flight. Give me five, and we can walk out together?"

"Let me use it before you get in." She scoots to the side and stands, then walks toward the bathroom. Once she closes the door, I stand and grab my bag from the closet that has my clothes. I pull out a pair of boxers, joggers, a t-shirt, and a sweat-shirt. I hear my phone buzz on the table and walk over and pick it up again. This time it's my mom. I'll answer her later too.

When Alie walks out of the bathroom, I nearly drop my clothes and take her to the bed again. She passes by me and starts to pick up her clothes off the floor.

"Hey, wait for me, yeah?" I lift my brows.

She nods. "I'll wait for you, but hurry up, Liam." A smile breaks out on her face.

"My name sure sounds good from your lips." I smile back at her and walk backward into the bathroom. I don't bother to shut the door.

CHAPTER
NINE

ALIE

I pull my red jumpsuit over my hips, the fabric sliding into place as softly as the knot forming in my chest. If I didn't already have plans today—and Liam didn't have to get back to New Orleans —I would've stayed tangled up with him in that bed until the very last possible second. Being wrapped around him felt dangerously easy.

Through the open crack of the bathroom door, I watch him step into the shower. Steam billows around the shape of his broad shoulders, the water carving paths along his skin until he disappears behind the fog. A smile tugs at my lips. Never in my life did I imagine I'd spend the night with *him*—Liam Pitz, one of the hottest new quarterbacks in the league. Of course, I knew who he was. I always know the players; it's impossible not to when you work in the business, and your father owns the New York Titans. But I didn't go to the wedding last night searching for him. I went because Aaron insisted I get out of my slump.

It's been a rough few months. My ex blindsided me in the fall, breaking up with me after pretending to care for nearly a year. It turned out he wasn't interested in me at all—just in getting close to my father. Another baller looking for a good time, as Dad put it. I learned the hard way that Grant girls need to tread carefully. Dad made me promise: no more athletes. Not for a while. Not until my judgment wasn't clouded by heart-break or loneliness.

So no, I didn't walk into the wedding plotting to fall headfirst into the arms of a rookie quarterback. In fact, Dad's played the warning on repeat my whole life: rookie athletes have terrible reputations—money, women, partying, football as their entire world. And when Liam told me he wasn't ready for a family, none of it surprised me. It fit exactly what Dad drilled into us: *Do not get mixed up with a man whose entire future depends on keeping his life uncomplicated.*

But then Liam smiled at me. Really smiled. And once we started talking about ridiculous things like being in a Christmas snow globe, something in me cracked open. He wasn't trying to charm me because of my last name. He didn't even know my last name. For the first time in a long time, someone saw *me*, not the Grant legacy or the Titans heiress. He looked at me like I was just a woman in a red dress, making him laugh. And once we were talking, I didn't want it to end.

Maybe that's why I let myself fall into his bed. Against my better judgment. Against every warning I've ever gotten. I don't know what I expected when I woke up here this morning, wrapped in his arms, listening to the low, sleepy rumble of his voice. But for a second—just a second—I wondered if this could be something more.

"What have I gotten myself into?" I whisper.

As if on cue, Liam's phone buzzes on the nightstand.

"Hey, Liam!" I call. "Your phone is ringing."

"It's fine—just ignore it," he says over the rush of water.

I try. I swear I do. But it keeps buzzing, persistently enough to draw my attention to the screen. When the name flashes across it. *Sabine.* My breath hitches. A woman's name. Elegant.

Familiar in a way that sends a quick, sharp sting up my spine. Jealousy flares, then fizzles, leaving humiliation simmering beneath it. I shouldn't care. I have no claim on him. But the truth is, a tiny piece of me already does.

The buzzing stops. I exhale, shrug into my coat. Then the phone lights up again.

Scott Jackson.

I know him. Everyone in football knows him—one of the top agents in the business—Liam's agent.

> Scott Jackson: No can do. You're in New Orleans for at least two more years per your contract. Put in the work and keep them happy with their decision to make you one of the highest-paid rookies in your class.

Two years in New Orleans.

Two years far away from New York.

Far away from me.

The small, reckless hope I didn't want to name flickers and dims.

Another buzz.

> Sabine: I didn't sleep at all last night. I need you.

My throat tightens. Another buzz.

> Sabine: I took a test this morning. I think I might be pregnant. The doctor said Tuesday is the earliest they can confirm. I want you with me... I shouldn't have to do this alone.

A wave of nausea rolls through me. Another buzz.

> Sabine: We can tell my family when you come home with me for the holidays.

The air in the room shifts—thick and heavy, pressing down on my ribs. This isn't a pleading ex. This is someone who speaks like she has a right to him.

Someone he made promises to.

My hands tremble as I stare at the screen. Every warning my father has ever thrown at me roars to the surface at once. Rookie athletes. Unreliable. Immature. Too many women. Too many blurred lines. Too many complications.

The room tilts.

This is not a fling he forgot to mention.

This is a man with someone waiting for him in New Orleans... someone who expects him at a doctor's appointment.

Someone who talks like he belongs to her.

And I... I'm the girl he met at a wedding. The girl in red, who he flirted with for one magical night. The girl who let herself believe he saw *her* and not her last name.

Because I have to add insult to injury, I see a notification from Archie Griffith. Of course, I scroll up to see it.

> Archie: Since I didn't hear back from you last night, I assume you got that pussy.

I am such an idiot. Everything inside me recoils at once. The memories of my ex. The warnings from my father. The constant fear of being used. The reality is that Liam lives in another state and now may have a child with someone who sounds very much like his girlfriend.

A painful, familiar thought slices through me:

I was stupid to believe, for even a second, that he could want me for me.

I look toward the bathroom door, steam drifting out beneath it, and every instinct inside me fractures. I should wait. I should ask. I should let him explain. But humiliation grips me tight. Fear grips me tighter.

My phone buzzes from somewhere in the room. I grab it

instinctively and shove it into my pocket, only for something small and hard to clink against it.

I pull it out. The ornament. The tiny Christmas tree we bought last night after wandering through Manhattan like two idiots high on winter air and each other.

It feels unbearably heavy now.

I set it beside his phone—both symbols of two worlds I can't be a part of.

My feet carry me to the door, even as my heart tries to root me in place. I pause with my hand on the handle, staring back at the bathroom. I almost call his name. Almost ask him what all this means. Almost choose to trust him.

But believing in people is how I got hurt last time. And I can't—*will not*—go through that again. Not with someone I could fall for. Not with someone whose life, career, and complications exist so far outside my reach.

I swallow hard, open the door, and whisper, "Goodbye, Blitzen."

Because if I say it any louder, I'll stay.

And staying might break me.

CHAPTER
TEN

LIAM

I hear a door close, and I look out into the room and don't see her. I wipe the water off my face and clear the glass to see better. "Alie?"

No response.

"What the fuck?" I turn off the water and grab a clean towel from the bar next to the shower. "Alie!" I yell out louder.

I don't bother drying off, but I wrap the towel around my waist and run into the room.

She's gone.

I jog over to the door and pull it open. The hallway is empty. "Goddamn it!"

How is this possible? She said she would wait for me. I know I didn't imagine what happened last night and again this morning. I step back into the room, and the door slams behind me.

I look around the room, looking for any sign of her. Maybe she had to leave, and she left me her number. But the only evidence of her being here are the rumpled bed sheets and the

Rockefeller Christmas Tree ornament she had picked out last night that sits on the small table next to my phone. "Fuck." I sit down in one of the chairs and lean my head back, resting on the chair.

Maybe I was just a fling to her after all.

EPILOGUE
EIGHT WEEKS LATER

ALI

I pace my small bathroom in my office as the timer on my phone winds down to zero. I close my eyes and take a deep breath in. As I exhale, I open my eyes and look down at the long white stick resting on the counter next to the sink.

Two pink lines.

"Oh. Fuck."

TO BE CONTINUED...

WHAT'S NEXT

Liam & Alie's story continues in The Trade (March 2026)!

What to expect: Professional Football, Second Chance, Found Family, No Love Triangle, oh…and a two year time jump.

Read on for a sneak peek inside Counter Play (Beck & Charlie) from the Walker University Stallions series!

COUNTER PLAY
SNEAK PEEK

CHARLIE

"CHARLIE!" my mother calls from the bottom of the stairs. "Are you about ready to go?"

I zip up my duffel bag and look around my childhood bedroom and sigh.

From the time I was a little girl, my parents always talked about Casey and me attending Walker University. He and I had big ideas about what we wanted to be when we grew up, and we thought we could fulfill those aspirations at Walker. Granted, it *was* where our parents had met and gone to school.

When we were little, I wanted to be a waitress while Casey wanted to be a professional football player. He's had a football in his hands since the day he was born. However, my plan of becoming a waitress quickly died. I tried it in high school, and let's just say, it did *not* live up to my expectations. Casey's dream, well, he's still living it—or he's on his way by playing football at the college level.

Casey went on to become a Walker University legacy. I, however, strayed from the family plan and went to another school.

I followed my friend Britney Stevens to Chandler State University. We had been close since middle school. Once I had gotten boobs and started to get noticed by boys other than Beck, she'd wanted to hang out. So, when we reached our senior year, she literally begged me to go to State with her, saying how great our college years would be together. It took a lot of coaxing, but I eventually caved, especially since my entire life had imploded that year.

Unfortunately, my freshman year of college at Chandler State University didn't turn out exactly the way I had planned.

Britney and I decided to room together, and to say things were tense from the beginning would be an understatement. For someone who was so adamant that I not go to Walker, it was as if once I was at State, she didn't have a use for me anymore. She quickly found a group of friends and often left me behind. I tried to settle in and even joined a sorority and dated a frat guy, Tony Pastorelli, for a while. I made some friends and did okay on my own for the first time in my life. Still, it never felt right.

Britney and I had a falling-out at the end of our freshman year, details of which I try not to think about, and it firmly solidified my decision to transfer. Her manipulation and her mind games were just too much for me to handle—which, looking back, I hadn't recognized in high school, but it'd become blatantly obvious in college. And I resented her for making me choose between her and my brother and my intention to go to Walker.

My family couldn't understand why I'd chosen to go to college with Brit instead of my brother. And even though he didn't say it, I knew Casey was disheartened that I wasn't going to be with him. It was the first time we would be separated for really any period of time. Sure, we'd each gone to sleepovers, and he'd gone off to football camp, but we'd never actually lived apart. I missed him terribly. I did visit him a few times, but it was too hard for me to be around Beck. When it got really bad with Britney and I broke up with Tony, I spent a lot of weekends at home.

So, this year, I'm transferring to Walker, and I can't wait to start this new chapter and be there to support my brother. Casey is a wide receiver and has worked really hard to make the starting lineup this season.

With one last look around my room and one final count of three switches of the light on my desk, I grab my bag and head down the stairs.

"Casey is waiting outside for you," Mom says as I round the landing.

"I still think it's unfair that we have to share the truck," I huff.

"Honey, he's right around the corner from you. I'm sure if you need the truck, you can grab it." She wraps her arm around mine when I reach her at the bottom of the stairs.

Casey lives in a house off campus with some of the other players on the team. She's right; it's not that far from the house I'll be living in. And luckily, the Walker campus is easy to walk around even though it's big. But still, that means I have to go over to his house and potentially run into Beck. Which is really the bigger problem.

My dad is waiting near the door. As we walk up to him, he reaches out to grab my duffel from my hand, and Mom lets go of my arm.

"Thanks, Dad. I'm going to miss you guys, but we'll see you in a few weeks for the opening game."

"Yes, your mom and I will be there early that day, so if you want to ride with us to the game, let us know, and we'll pick you up," he says while putting his other arm around me as we walk out the door.

"You sure you have everything you need?" Mom asks.

"Yeah, I think so. If I forgot anything, I'll have you bring it when you come to campus."

"Okay, that works," she says. "I know you're going to roll

your eyes at me when I say this, but I feel much better about you going to Walker with Casey and Beck than I did when you left for State with Britney last year. You know she was never my favorite."

At the mention of Beck, my heart sinks. "I know, and I agree. I feel much better about this year overall. I have a better handle for what I want to specialize in too. I feel like psychology is a good route for me. And I'll admit, it was hard, being away from Casey last year. Twins have to stay together—ya feel me?" I say with a laugh.

Rolling her eyes, she says, "Yes, I feel you. Just please keep an eye on each other and make good choices."

I love to tease my mom, so I can't help but say, "Mother, I promise we will make very good *bad* choices; don't worry."

She shakes her head as we walk up to the truck. "Casey, please keep your sister in line. But seriously, I love you both. Have an amazing year, and we'll see you in just a few weeks. Call us when you get there. Oh, and, Charlie, don't forget to call Aunt Linds when you get closer to campus so she can meet you at the sorority house with your room key."

"Okay. Yeah, I have a reminder set on my phone to call her. I'm just glad they could fit me into the house so I don't have to live in the dorms this year."

My mom was in a sorority in college, which I really didn't think would be my thing, but she made some really great life-long friends, so that's why I rushed last year at Chandler State. And because I was a legacy, it was really just a formality. I'm really glad I did it, given how things ended up with Brit. Now it will also make my transition to Walker easier because I already know a few of the girls in the house. One is Lindsay's daughter, Arbor, and the other is her roommate, Lily. Plus, the house is a freaking mansion.

Lindsay Gibbs—who I refer to as Aunt Linds—and my mom met their freshman year at Walker. They rushed together and have been friends ever since. She's the alumni chair for the sorority, so she basically keeps all the girls in line and helps manage the operations of the house.

"Aunt Linds is practically family. You know she always has your back," Mom says as she gives my hand a squeeze. "Aren't you a little sad you missed the rush festivities? I always had so much fun, making the skits and dances."

I turn to look at her with a *you've got to be kidding me* " expression on my face, but when I see her smile is genuine, I just smile and nod. "Maybe next year."

Casey has nothing to load into the truck since he's been at school for over a month now for training. He just decided to come up to get me instead of Mom and Dad taking me.

Dad hands Casey my duffel bag and he loads the last of my things into the back of the truck bed when he says, "Charlie, you need to ride in the back."

"No, sir. Why?" I ask.

"Because I'm sitting in the front," Beckham's deep voice booms as he crosses the street and reaches the truck.

Fuck.

When I turn, I make eye contact with Beckham, and he gives me a snarky look. I just huff and shake my head.

I hear Mom and Dad talking, but I can't really focus on what they're saying. I mean, it's kind of hard to when I have the intense eyes of my ex-boyfriend staring me down.

Literally.

Beckham Linson—the one I once loved fiercely before our relationship shattered into a million pieces. It's been two years since we were a couple, and the pain of the fallout still stings despite the fact that he's remained Casey's best friend and my parents' second son.

I've done everything I could to stay away from him. My heart is still attached to the memories, and my body betrays me when I look at him. Beck—with his stupid-hot blue eyes that are nearly gray and his brown hair that's almost black—sort of has the whole Clark Kent–looking thing going, minus the glasses. The look he has right before he rips open his shirt and looks all hot and shit. And his height—the only way I can match his six-foot frame is if I'm on stairs or something. He's no longer a teenage boy. He's a man.

A man I will see a lot more of now that we'll both be at Walker. Beckham is the starting running back for the football team. He was recruited heavily by Walker to play football, so he was able to earn a starting spot on the team, even as a freshman.

Between him being Casey's best friend and a star athlete on campus, there's no way I'm going to be able to avoid him.

I hear Mom say one last goodbye, and I head toward the front seat of the truck anyway. Completely ignoring my brother's order. Right as I'm reaching for the handle, Beckham comes up behind me, crowding me against the door.

That imposing frame of his blocks me in, and I can feel the heat of his skin burning through his T-shirt and smell the fresh scent of the cologne he's worn since our freshman year of high school. It was originally a gift from me. I'm actually a little surprised he still wears it, but I can't say it doesn't give me a little bit of satisfaction.

"There's no way I'm sitting in the back. You get back there," he drawls.

Luckily, I've become immune to his good looks and broody charm, which have everyone in this town—other than me—falling at his feet.

"Are you kidding me right now, Beckham? You know I get carsick." *I mean, it's a double-cab truck, and it's a beast, so I probably won't get carsick, but I'm going for it anyway.*

"That's not really my problem, Charlene."

Casey looks over at us and grunts, "Are you two at it already? Can't you call a truce for the two-hour ride? Charlie, you know Beckham can't fit in the back seat. His legs are too

long. Just try to deal with it. Put your headphones on and tune out the noise or read your book. Anything to make it a chill ride. I can't deal with you two fighting the whole way."

Beckham still has me crowded up against the door, so I finally turn around to face him. He has a smirk on his face, knowing he's won this round. He's still not backing up, so I have to put my hands on his chest and push him away, which makes him laugh even more.

I reach out to pull the handle of the rear cab when Beck beats me to it. "I've got it. I don't need your help, Beckham."

"Oh, but it's my pleasure, Charlene."

I throw my bag in, step up onto the sideboard, and pull myself up into the massive truck, using the oh-shit handle. I've had to use it many times, so we're well acquainted. Casey and Beckham like to go off-roading in this truck, even though it makes my mom crazy. It's massive and pretty freaking awesome. But it's a pain in the ass to get in and out of. Especially for me. I think my brother took all the tall genes when we were in the womb.

Beckham is still smirking at me as I grab the door handle and pull the door shut.

This is going to be a bitch of a ride.

ACKNOWLEDGMENTS

To my family, thank you for your support. You're my reason for everything. I love you all, eternally. Merry Christmas!

Compass Press, thank you for walking me through the author journey.

Jovanna Shirley, once again, thank you for your patience and expertise. Only a few days off this time. Please keep me around!

Jeannine Colette, this book is for you. You have championed Liam from day one, and I couldn't thank you enough for helping me get this ready to shine.

Sarah Sentz, I don't know where to start. The value you add to the team...I have no words. I hope you know how grateful we are to have you. P.S., you can't escape us. Ever.

Sam R, thank you for reading early. I love seeing your messages and your love for the series means the world to me.

Rickie, thank you so much for reading. Your video, after reading, made me laugh so hard!

To my ARC Team and all readers, thank you for reading more of my words! Your reviews, edits, and just knowing you're reading still blow my mind. Thank you, thank you!

Wordsmith Publicity, Autumn and Roxie, thank you for helping me reach readers and for your guidance and support!

ABOUT THE AUTHOR

Ava Sutton is a sports enthusiast and author of spicy college and professional sports romance.

When she's not writing, you can find her nose in a book, scrolling social media or planning dream vacations she someday hopes to take. She lives in Dallas, Texas with her two dogs. Connect with her on Facebook, Instagram, and TikTok. @avasuttonbooks

www.avasuttonbooks.com